THE SPOTTED DOG

To Rosemary —
Best Wishes
Nancy Winslow Parker
Los Angeles   1983

THE SPOTTED DOG

The Strange Tale of a Witch's Revenge

Written and illustrated by

Nancy Winslow Parker

DODD, MEAD & COMPANY · NEW YORK

Copyright © 1980 by Nancy Winslow Parker
All rights reserved
No part of this book may be reproduced in any form
without permission in writing from the publisher
Printed in the United States of America

First Edition

Library of Congress Cataloging in Publication Data

Parker, Nancy Winslow.
The spotted dog.

SUMMARY: By not following the witch's instructions
a family's lives are deeply affected.
[1. Witches—Fiction] I. Title.
PZ7.P2274Sp   [E]   80–13363
ISBN 0–396–07845–1

This book is dedicated
to
Loretta Howard,
friend and inspiration

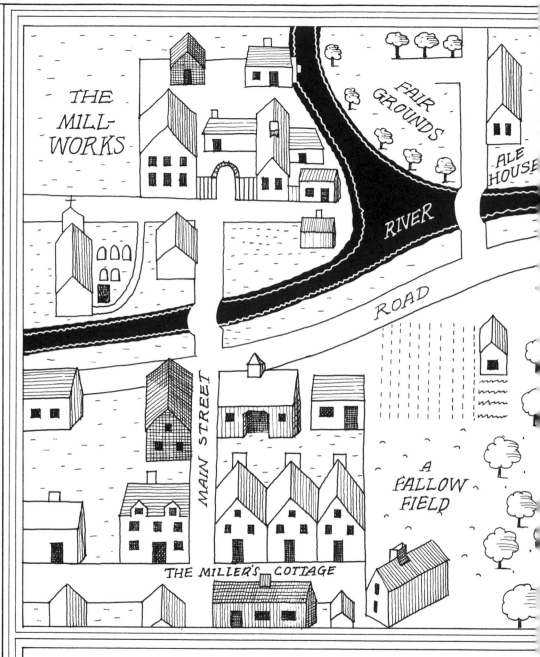

THE VILLAGE OF WALLHORN, INCLUDING THE
CRUIKSHANK-JONES ESTATE, AS IT APPEARED

THE QUARRY

N
W   E
S

ROAD

THE
WOODS

THE
CRUIKSHANK-
JONES ESTATE

MILLWORKS, WOODS AND FIELDS, AND THE
AROUND THE TURN OF THE CENTURY.   NWP

THE SPOTTED DOG

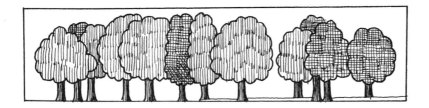

Prologue

ONCE UPON A TIME there lived in a village near a dark woods, an aristocratic and proud family named Cruikshank-Jones. Mr. Cruikshank-Jones owned a large mill where he worked very hard. The mill had been built along a rushing river many years ago by Mr. Cruikshank-Jones's grandfather, who harnessed the river's waters into power to drive the mill's machinery. The mill flourished and provided jobs for most of the people who lived in the village, which was called Wallhorn. Mrs. Cruikshank-Jones spent her days in the garden, and in bad weather by the fireplace occupied in needlework. They had two children, a boy Freddy, and Eileen, a toddler. In the servants' hall of the mill owner's house there was a cook, a chambermaid, and a nursemaid to take care of baby Eileen.

It has been said in the village that Freddy Cruikshank-Jones was born on the dark side of the moon,
which might have been the reason why he was forget-

ful and sometimes disobedient. It is more likely that his character stemmed from his independence of mind and spirit. Nevertheless, it was probably a combination of all these things which nearly brought about the ruin of the proud family Cruikshank-Jones.

The most important thing to remember about the misfortune that befell the family was the day when Freddy and his dog, a handsome Dalmatian profusely marked with liver-colored spots, were walking home from the village. The Cruikshank-Joneses' house, built along the same river that flowed by the mill owned by Mr. Cruikshank-Jones, was about three miles outside the village. It could be reached from the main road, an easy hour's walk, but a hot and dusty one in the summertime. The other way to the house was across a fallow field and through the woods, which took half the time. However, no one had been in the woods for many years and it had become dark and tangled with wild growth. The rumors that a half-crazed cart driver had strangled his wife there in a fit of jealousy over twenty years ago had put many people off ever entering the woods again.

13

Chapter One

ON THIS PARTICULAR DAY, which was hot and sultry, Freddy Cruikshank-Jones decided, for some reason which has never been fully explained, to take the short cut through the woods to his house. Perhaps Freddy thought it would be cooler in the forbidding woods. In any event, he left the main road slightly north of the miller's cottage, cut across the fallow field, and entered the woods with his dog, Major, at his heels. They had not gone very far when Freddy regretted his action, for the woods were very still and the path was full of rocks and twisted roots. The sharp, pungent odor of decaying leaves and rotting tree trunks hung in the heavy summer air. But the boy kept on, too stubborn to turn around and go back by the longer, safer route.

They were about one-third of the way into the woods when Freddy came upon an old woman sitting by the side of the path. A midnight blue raven perched

on a branch over her head. She was oddly dressed for the heat in many layers of brown skirts, and wore a blouse in the Elizabethan style with huge puffed sleeves. On her head was a dusty, dark green hat, and her bare feet had seen neither soap nor water for a very long time. She was holding a leather satchel with a lock that gleamed like gold in the forest shadows.

"Good day to you," said the old woman.

"Good day to you, old woman," said the boy.

"What are you doing in these woods, young man?"

"I'm on my way home. I thought I'd cut through the woods as the way is shorter. I must get Major ready for the big dog show at the village fair tomorrow. I don't have much time."

"Why have you waited so long to groom your dog?" asked the old woman.

Although it was becoming darker and gloomier in the woods with each passing minute, and Freddy should have been home long ago, he paused to answer the old woman.

"I guess I have been too busy," he said.

"Well, just what do you have to do to the dog? He looks fine to me," snapped the old woman, squinting through the long shadows. "One dog is as good as another."

It was obvious to Freddy that the old woman knew nothing at all about dog shows.

"The dog's skin is scratched and torn from chasing through the thorny underbrush, and his paws are cut from running across the sharp rocks at the quarry. He is very dirty too. It will take more than one bath to get him clean enough to enter the show ring."

Warming up to his favorite subject, Freddy went on to tell the old woman that judges generally overlook the cuts and scratches a hunting dog may incur in the honorable pursuit of game, and look instead for clearness of eye and the carriage of the tail. But, still, Freddy felt uneasy about entering a scratched-up dog in the show ring.

"Some dogs in the village never go into the fields and get scratched or dirty. They have sleek coats, and one of them may very well win the prize," said Freddy.

"Alas, I will do the best I can with him tonight and hope for the best."

The old woman listened attentively.

"Major is the son and grandson of champions. He *must* win tomorrow," the boy added boldly.

The old woman thought awhile and finally got up and walked around the boy and dog three times. Then she sat down and poked at the golden lock on the leather bag with her finger. The bag flew open and an ivory brush popped out and into her lap. The bristles were soft as a baby's skin and the handle was curved like a hunter's horn.

"This is what you must do to win the prize," said the old woman, getting up again and shaking the ivory brush under Freddy's nose.

"Wash the dog with the brush tonight, but wash nothing else. Tell no one about the brush. When you are through with the brush, wrap it in a linen handkerchief and bury it in the garden at once. Now run home and do as I have told you."

The boy promised to obey. He put the brush in his

pocket and thanked the old woman. Then he and the dog ran the rest of the way through the woods and were soon home with his mother and father and baby Eileen.

That night after dinner, the boy prepared the dog's bath. He was very excited and moved quickly around the room. First, he poured water in the tub, then he carefully lifted the dog into the warm water. He put

the ivory brush the old woman had given him in the water with the dog, and finally got in the tub too, for that was how he always bathed his dog.

The dog sensed the importance of the occasion and for once was still while the boy scrubbed him all over with the brush. His white coat glistened like silver and the liver-colored spots, scattered randomly over the handsome dog, became a deeper and richer brown than they had ever been. As the soft bristles of the brush moved around the dog's face, his eyes became brighter and clearer than a new penny, and a brief scrub of the magnificent paws restored them instantly to their former firmness. The boy brushed on, splashing water all over in his exuberance, and finally, deliberately ignoring the old woman's words, he scrubbed himself from head to toe with the little ivory brush. Then he stepped out of the tub, and dried and dressed himself. Finally, he rubbed the dog dry with a towel, tossed the ivory brush in the corner of the room, and went to bed. He fell fast asleep, his beloved spotted dog at his feet.

Chapter Two

THE NEXT MORNING THE BOY awoke and jumped out of bed, for it was the day of the big dog show at the village fair—the Exhibition and Field Trials which came but once a year. The first thing Freddy did was call for his dog, and you can imagine his surprise when a strange, all-white dog answered his familiar voice.

However, the usual affectionate greeting was cut short as the dog drew back in astonishment at his master whose body was covered with large, liver-colored spots.

Freddy tore off his nightshirt and stood in front of the mirror. There was no doubt about it—Freddy Cruikshank-Jones was covered from head to toe with the distinguished markings of an English coaching dog.

Freddy dressed slowly and carefully, trying to hide the spots. He put on a long-sleeved shirt and the longest summer pants he owned, which unfortunately came only to his knees. Then he went downstairs and,

with heavy heart, took his place at the breakfast table where his father and mother were finishing their toast and marmalade.

It is extremely painful to relate the emotional scene which followed the first shock Mr. and Mrs. Cruik-shank-Jones suffered when they saw their son at the breakfast table, sporting the markings on his face and ears of their pet dog, and the near breakdown of the couple when the dog, now dazzling white, came into the room.

24

Somehow, the mortified boy found his tongue and told his mother and father about the old woman in the woods and the ivory brush she had given him to use in the dog's bath.

"Wicked, hateful old witch! To do this to my child!" cried Mrs. Cruikshank-Jones.

"Nasty old hag! She deserves to be hanged," thundered the father.

When their anger had somewhat subsided, Mr. and Mrs. Cruikshank-Jones decided they would all go to the woods and confront the old woman who had done this dreadful thing to their son, and make her undo her mischief. And leaving baby Eileen with the nursemaid, Mother and Father Cruikshank-Jones, their spotted son Freddy, and his all-white Dalmatian went into the woods to find the old witch.

Chapter Three

THE FAMILY HAD NOT WALKED very far into the woods when they came upon the old woman dressed in the many layers of brown skirts, the puffy-sleeved blouse, and with the dusty green hat pulled down over her stringy black hair. She was sitting by the path and had a large tin box next to her with a silver lock which shone mysteriously in the dim forest. The raven, sitting on the old woman's shoulder, flapped noisily into the trees as the Cruikshank-Joneses approached.

Without waiting to say "Good day" or "How are you?" the elder Cruikshank-Jones burst upon her in a rage and threatened to have her strung up by her heels if she did not remove the spots at once from their son and put them back on the dog where they belonged. And Mr. Cruikshank-Jones went on, in a voice that echoed throughout the forest, saying that his son's heart had been set on winning at the village dog show. It was a point of honor with the family to compete fiercely, if necessary, in the show ring among those who fancied this particular breed. And now this unspeakable witch had played a most hideous prank on the boy.

The witch appeared unimpressed.

"Is this how you repay my kindness?" she replied. "I gave the boy a fine brush, the proper use of which would cause all the prizes in the world to fall at his feet. He has shown his gratitude by disobeying every instruction. Now you see what happens when people do not keep their promises."

"Indeed, it is as the old woman says," the boy confessed. "I ignored what she told me to do, for I didn't think it important."

By now the sun was fairly high and the time for the competition was drawing close.

"See here, old woman," said the father impatiently. "The boy is truly sorry he failed to keep his promise. Now I will pay you handsomely if you will only restore my son and the dog to their original complexions." Then the mill owner took all the gold he had in his pockets and held it out to the old hag.

The witch got up and waved aside the mill owner's hand. She walked slowly around the boy and dog three times. Then, leaning over, she poked the silver lock on the tin box with her bony finger and the lid flew back and a little cup popped out. She took from the box several small crystal bottles which contained colored liquids, and pouring a mixture of them into the little cup, stirred it vigorously with a wooden spoon. Then she commanded the boy to drink the mixture. No sooner had he swallowed the last drop, when he and his dog were at once restored to their original colors—the boy a ruddy pink and the dog with his rich dark spots.

The witch gave the boy the spoon and told him to use it at every meal for the next seven days.

"Now off with you and do not forget my instructions. I warn you, there is a limit to the times one may be forgiven."

The boy thanked the witch and left the woods with his family. They walked the rest of the way to the village, getting there barely in time for the dog show. And just as the old woman had promised, the spotted dog far outshone his competitors and won a blue ribbon and a large silver plate.

The Cruikshank-Joneses left the fair just as the sun was setting below the hills, and walked home along the river. Mrs. Cruikshank-Jones was silent during the walk, and appeared to be brooding over something on her mind.

"With all my heart," the mother finally said to her son, "I wish you would never go into the woods again, and neither speak nor have anything whatever to do with that terrible old witch. And I forbid you to use that spoon she gave you. I want to be rid of her and her tricks forever." And saying this, Mrs. Cruikshank-Jones grabbed the spoon from her little son's hand and, despite the boy's protests, impulsively threw it into the river. Freddy watched in horror as the witch's little wooden spoon bobbed around for awhile in the water, before being caught in a current and swept out to sea.

Chapter Four

WHEN THE PROUD FAMILY Cruikshank-Jones
came home that evening—mother, father, son, and
their champion dog Major—they burst into the nursery to show baby Eileen the ribbon and the silver plate
won at the village fair.

It is difficult to believe what followed, but the cook
later repeated in the village what she had seen and one
cannot discredit her firsthand observations. It seems
that upon entering the room, the first thing the family
saw was the nursemaid weeping at the baby's crib. In-
side the crib was a little brown terrier with wagging

tail, barking at the nursemaid. She held an ivory brush in her hand and on her lap was a damp towel.

When she finally stopped crying and dried her swollen eyes, she told them that at dusk, just as the sun was setting behind the hills, she was washing baby Eileen in the tub when, out of the corner of her eye, she saw an ivory brush on the floor. She picked it up and brushed baby Eileen all over with the soft little bristles. When the baby's bath was over, she wrapped her in a towel and took her back to the nursery, but when she unwound the towel in the crib, there was this little brown terrier, and not a trace of baby Eileen. Then the nursemaid started to cry again and had to be helped to the servants' hall by the cook, who had been drawn to the nursery by all the noise.

Chapter Five

FREDDY'S MOTHER TOOK the news more calmly than those who were close to her expected. She went on doing fancy needlework, rarely leaving the garden or house to go to the village, and retained the nursemaid to take care of the little brown terrier with the same love and affection she had previously given baby Eileen.

Freddy's father made several inquiries in the village about the old witch and offered a reward to anyone who could find her. But the villagers were no help and were more frightened than ever to enter the woods. He finally gave up and threw himself deeper into his work at the mill.

Freddy and his dog Major roamed the open fields around the house, flushing game from the underbrush and chasing hare and fox near the stone quarry. They never once saw the old woman who wore the many layers of brown skirts, the puffy-sleeved blouse, and the dusty green hat. They did play a lot with the little brown terrier, who loved to run and nip at the spotted dog's legs. At times, it crossed Freddy's mind that he might enter the little brown terrier in the next dog show in the village.

Chapter Six

Several years went by after the ghastly occurrence at the mill owner's house. The nursemaid, a dutiful and simple lass, accepted her new responsibilities with a willing spirit and grew to love the little brown terrier as if it had been her own child.

As for the little terrier, a female, she grew into a fine compact dog with all the characteristics of her breed—the erect ears, short muzzle, and hard wiry coat. She was the epitome of excellence; seldom had a more perfect example of this particular terrier been seen in that part of the country for many, many years. All this, of course, was lost on the elder Cruikshank-

Joneses, for they saw only grief when they looked on the little dog and yearned instead for their missing baby Eileen.

But Freddy Cruickshank-Jones had a keen eye for animals, and one evening he asked his mother and father if he could enter the little brown terrier in the dog show at the village fair the next day.

The mother and father yielded to their son's wishes, for they knew the boy was fond of the animal, and now being their only child, they begrudged him no pleasures. However, they declined to go with him to the show, as the memories from the last fair were too painful to relive.

So, late that night after everyone had gone to bed, Freddy gave the little brown terrier a bath. He wet her body all over with foaming soapsuds and, holding her still with one hand, he reached into his pocket

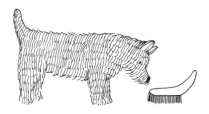

with the other hand and pulled out the little ivory brush! It was the same brush the witch had given him and which he had hidden in his closet all these years.

With trembling hands, Freddy scrubbed the dog from end to end, up and down the legs and around and around the neck and ears. When he had finished, Freddy crept down into the garden and, with the little dog watching, he wrapped the ivory brush in a linen handkerchief and buried it under a lilac bush.

A few minutes later, up in his room, Freddy tucked the little brown dog in the bed alongside the spotted dog and all went to sleep.

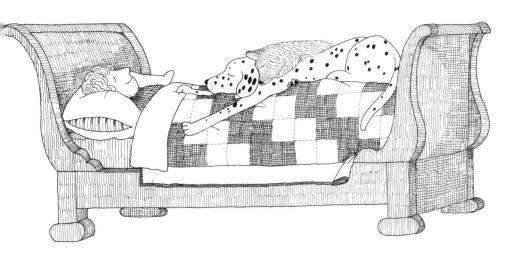

Chapter Seven

IT IS SUFFICIENT TO SAY that the little brown terrier won three ribbons and two silver cups at the dog show the next day. Never had such a fine dog been seen in the Wallhorn show ring, far outshining the champion Chow Chow with the blue-black tongue, who had never before been defeated in his life.

They went home directly after the show as Freddy was anxious to show his parents the prizes the little dog had won, hoping the success of the day would bring joy into their bitter lives.

But, alas, Mrs. Cruikshank-Jones was sadder than

ever at the sight of the ribbons and silver cups. Indeed, it seemed her heart would break as she took the little brown terrier in her arms. Burying her head in the dog's neck, she let her tears fall into its fur. At last,

she kissed the top of the dog's head and handed her to the waiting nursemaid. But suddenly the terrier wriggled free from her grasp, jumped to the floor, and ran out the open door into the garden.

It took a while for everyone to understand what had happened. Freddy rushed into the garden after the little dog, and was just in time to see it running across the lawn and heading for the woods. By the time the family reached the woods, the dog was nowhere in sight.

Everyone went in different directions, but it was Freddy who followed the path full of rocks and twisted roots. And at precisely the spot where a dark raven perched in the branches overhead he found the long lost baby Eileen—not a day older than when she had vanished from her crib a few years ago.

And although the family looked and looked in the woods, along the road, and in the garden, the little brown terrier was never seen again.

Epilogue

FREDDY WAS TERRIBLY disappointed that he never saw the little brown terrier again, for he had grown very fond of her. And he never went into the woods again—not that that sinister place held any singular fear for him, for he was a brave lad and capable of holding his own. Instead, he preferred to run with Major in the fields, chasing after game, exploring along the river, and wandering as far to the west as the village and the mill works.

At first, it was difficult not to tell his parents about the ivory brush buried in the garden, but as time went by, it became less and less of a strain and he almost forgot about the entire incident and the remarkable little brown terrier.

Freddy's mother, Mrs. Cruikshank-Jones, seemed to grow younger and younger every day and rarely had time to do the tiny stitches in her fancy needlework. Rather, she gave herself to the activities in the village, sponsoring countless parties and balls. And she never grew tired of showing her visitors the colorful ribbons and the silver cups her charming and beautiful daughter had won in the dog show.

Freddy's father worked harder than ever at the mill, improving the buildings, the yards, and the workers' pay. Every year he gave the mill hands a holiday on the anniversary of his daughter's reappearance.

And every year at the Exhibition and Field Trials —hereafter known as The Great Wallhorn Show— sportsmen came from all over the countryside with their hunters and retrievers, terriers and pointers, setters and other dogs to compete for the most coveted prize in all dogdom, the Cruikshank-Jones Golden Cup.

As for the nursemaid, she was asked to stay on at the house and take care of the growing baby Eileen, but for some reason, which everyone thought most ungrateful, she decided instead to find work in the village. She was last seen serving drinks in the alehouse not far from the fairgrounds.

The End

Written and illustrated by Nancy Winslow Parker

Illustrated by Nancy Winslow Parker